Crunchy Life

Every Point Counts

Written By

Glen Mourning

ISBN: 978-1-7172-6874-7

DEDICATION

In a world full of challenges, children may have it the hardest when it comes to learning how to make the most out of life. And when you are fortunate enough to make it from childhood to adulthood, remember that along the way, there were plenty of grown-ups who cared for you at times, more than you cared for yourself. This book is dedicated to all of the loving adults around the world who want the most out of life for the children that they serve. It truly takes a village to get these students of ours to see their full potential.

ACKNOWLEDGMENTS

To my mother, Lillian

Without your support and unconditional love, I would have indeed given up on myself as a young man and as a student. Attending school was challenging, but when I learned how education could open the door to a better tomorrow, I learned to wake up each morning with a purpose. You made me believe in me! Thank you to all of the fantastic parents, guardians, teachers, coaches and mentors around the world. Your efforts are necessary and appreciated.

Never give up.
Success is on the other side
of your struggle.

Reading Standard question stems for developing strong independent thinkers

Why did (event) happen? How do you know? •
What does (character) think about (event)? How
do you know? • What do you think (character)
will do differently next time? • Explain why
(character or object) is important to the story.

What happened at the beginning, middle, and end
of the story? • What is a summary of this story? •
What is the lesson you should learn from this
story? • What is this story trying to teach?

How does (character) feel at this part of the
story? How do you know? • How does
(character) actions change what happens in the
story? • What problem does (character) have in
the story? How does he/she solve their problem?
• How does (character) change throughout the
story? • What are (character) personality traits? How
does his/ her personality affect what happens in the
story? • Why is the setting important to the story?

How are the parts of the story connected? How does this section/chapter help the reader understand the setting? • How does this scene build suspense? • How would you retell this story, including important parts from the beginning, middle, and end? • In poetry what stanza is the most interesting to you? Why? • Why did the author organize the story like this? How would it be different if the order were changed?

Who is telling this story? How do you know? • Are the narrator and the author the same person? How do you know? • What point of view is this written from? • What does (character/narrator) think of (event/action)? What do you think? What would you have done differently?

Sometimes… life gets a little crunchy!

INTRODUCTION

Elite Public Charter School or EPCS, as it will often be referred to as, is a fictional charter school located in Washington, D.C. The characters and their families are based on real-life people and events.

Sometimes, life isn't as smooth or as safe as we would want it to be. Sometimes, life can get a little challenging, a little discouraging, and a little *crunchy*. Just keep on living and doing what you can to find success through all of the struggles. Just keep on chewing away. It'll always get better if you believe it will. Never give up hope.

CHAPTER ONE

Thinking back to the week before Mother's Day weekend, the kids in room 227 were incredibly excited and anxious about the Saturday before they would all have a chance to celebrate their mothers and grandmas. The end of the year progress report cards were also heading home that weekend to ensure that parents knew which students were heading

1

down the right path to have a smooth transition to middle school. It had appeared that Crunchy was turning his grades around, but with all of the attention that continued to overwhelm him, he was letting the fun and excitement of having been on TV distract him.

Student Name: Charles Anthony Thomas **Parent:** Ms. Amani Jones **Address:** 123 Alabama Avenue Southeast, Washington, D.C	**Grade 5** **May** **Progress** **Report Card**
Reading	D
Math	D
Social Studies	B
Science	C
P.E	A
Music	A
Art	A
Spanish	C

Comments and concerns	Parent signature required
This quarter we have been working on writing narrative summaries as well as identifying the elements of poetry. Students have read several texts that require them to effectively write summaries and identify components of narratives and poems that assist with comprehension. Charles is regularly practicing reading comprehension skills but is only slightly improving on high-frequency words on a 3rd-grade level. Currently, Charles is performing at the level of an average mid-year 3rd grader. At home, you can help Charles by encouraging him to read every night for 15-20 minutes and asking him to complete our weekly reading and writing homework.	_____ _____

During the middle of the week leading up to the big Mother's Day weekend, Crunchy had been more emotional than days in the past. Perhaps he knew that for some reason, he wasn't doing as best as he could be doing in

3

school. With all that was happening, somehow, he had managed to earn enough scholar dollars through being positively rewarded in classes to attend the spring ice cream social dance. He had managed to write a poem that was bragged about by his classmates and even by Mr. Leroy. And he had also managed to have more than one friendly conversation with his new friend Alyah.

But even with all of those positive things going on, Crunchy was still pretty sad during the first week of May. One afternoon, after getting home and finishing his big state test review activities, Crunchy decided to lay down on his grandma's bedroom floor.

Usually, Grandma Jones didn't allow the kids in her room, but as long as all of the cleaning was done and the TV and lights in the house were off, from time to time, she let a grandchild or two hang out in there with the door open.

"Hey grandma, I'm gonna lay down before I have to help my mom clean the bathroom. I'm not feeling that good," called out Crunchy.

Just like a light, Crunchy had laid down at the foot of his grandma's bed and was fast asleep.

When Crunchy woke up, it was still sunny outside. It had seemed as if he had only rested for about ten or fifteen minutes. But when Crunchy walked downstairs to the kitchen, the clock on the microwave read 6:30 am. Crunchy, knowing it had only been Wednesday when he took a nap, realized that it must have been Thursday morning, perfect timing to get his sisters ready for school.

But when Crunchy walked down the hall to poke his head into the family guest room where his two sisters slept side by side, they were nowhere to be found.

Crunchy thought to himself that they must have already started to prepare for school, so he traced his steps and went back into the kitchen. As Crunchy took his long, quiet steps to the kitchen in search of Nicole and Serenity, Crunchy could not believe his eyes. Sitting at the kitchen table was a man who Crunchy hadn't seen for years. Smiling from ear to ear, humming the tune of Crunchy's favorite Michael Jackson song was Mr. Noah Jones.

Crunchy's grandad was sitting in the kitchen, more alive than ever before. He was an older, dark brown man, with grey and black curly hair that was perfectly faded on the sides and lined up with a perfect line, which seemed like the doings of the best barber in D.C. His eyes were pearly white with bushy grey and black brows. The wrinkles in his forehead seemed to be placed at perfect distances from one another as if they had been intentionally designed on his face to give him beautiful, distinct features of wisdom and grace. And to top off his impressive appearance, he was wearing a gold tuxedo!

Crunchy was scared out of his mind. He was so unsure as to who he was seeing, better yet, what he was seeing, that he almost screamed out loud in fear and panic.

"Charles...ha..ha...come on ova' and give yo' grandaddy a big ole' hug, ya understand," quietly called out Grandad Jones.

At the sound of Granda Jones' voice, all of the fear and confusion that Crunchy was feeling had disappeared as he jumped into his grandad's arms, crying tears of joy and happiness.

"But...you...you...but--" cried out Crunchy.

Before he could finish his sentence, Grandad Jones interrupted Crunchy.

"Don't worry, Charles, everything is just fine. I hope you doin' what you need to be doin' in school. Oh, and you gonn' go to Howard when you older, ain't that right? Never mind that for now, son. How about we cook us up some of that good ole' breakfast you used to love eating with me. Oh, and before we're done, I'll finally teach you how to make my famous sweet potato pie. Oh yeah...your momma and grandma just love my sweet potato pie, one tablespoon of brown sugar. How about it," asked Grandad Jones.

Still trying to understand how this was possible, Crunchy let go of the confusion about how his grandad, who had been gunned down by a man a few years ago, was now alive, living and breathing in the kitchen.

As if the tragic moment never happened, the two of them took out all of the ingredients and foods that they needed to make the best breakfast ever. Only one thing was missing, so Crunchy grabbed the eggs from out of the refrigerator. And with a swift, salsa dancer-like grace, his grandad spun around the refrigerator door to the cabinet to grab the pan.

While the two of them sang their favorite Michael Jackson song, they twirled and slid around the kitchen, arranging more on the countertops; grits, pancake mix, syrup, and sausages. They continued to dance. They continued to swirl around and sing, all while smiling, dancing, and preparing what was sure to be the best-tasting food ever.

When the cooking was over, and the two of them sat down, there had still been no sign of

Serenity or Nicole or Grandma Clara or Ms. Jones. It seemed as if the gentlemen had the entire house to themselves.

The food finished cooking, and they sat down to eat. "Hey, buddy...would you mind if I bless the food for us," suggested Grandad Jones.

Crunchy didn't hesitate to nod his head in agreement.

"Oh, Father God, you are a good, good father to Charles, to his sisters, to his mother, and to my wife. You see them trying to do their best in school, and you know how hard my two babies are working to raise Charles, Serenity, and Nicole. Continue to bless them and keep them out of harm's way. Amen"

As Grandad Jones finished his prayer, the two of them ate and laughed and joked and ate some more. Crunchy filled his grandad in on his new teacher Mr. Leroy and Crunchy shared the news about having been on TV for working hard during Black History Month. Crunchy also snuck in an update of his big cousin Rae'Anna and shared with Grandad Jones how she was teaching him all about college and all about HBCUs.

And as promised, Grandad Jones showed Crunchy exactly how to make his famous sweet potato pie. While Grandad Jones finished explaining what the final ingredient was to make the pie taste just perfect, he stopped to share one more thought with his grandson.

"You know, Charles. When I was ten-years-old, I was finally old enough to play in the Southeast Mother's Day basketball tournament. It's been going on for as long as I can ever remember. And one thing that I wish I was going to be able to do was coach you and the boys in the neighborhood so that we could bring another championship to the Jones' House," reminisced Grandad Jones.

Crunchy had heard stories of how his grandad was a legendary black-top basketball player who had almost gone on to play professional basketball after graduating from Howard University.

The story has it that Noah Jones was one of the best basketball players that Washington, D.C had ever known. But when it came time to choose between the NBA or sticking around to help raise his family, Granda Jones chose to stay home with a pregnant Mrs. Jones who was about to have her first baby, Crunchy's mother.

Crunchy had never known about the Mother's Day basketball tournament. And in that moment, he had realized that his grandad, who had wished that he could coach Crunchy and his friends around the neighborhood, would never get the chance to do so.

Crunchy, full off of the best breakfast food he had ever had, told his grandad that he would wash the dishes.

Unprepared for what would happen next, as Crunchy reached for the plate that his grandad had in his hand, just as fast as it had all taken place, Crunchy's dream of spending a morning with his granda was over.

CHAPTER TWO

Startled and gasping for air, Crunchy woke up from his nap, reaching out his hand, only to find the foot of his grandma's bed at the other end of his stretched out arms. Neatly folded and covering where he had reached out and touched was a blanket that had been in Crunchy's family for decades.

"Crunchy," shouted Ms. Jones. "Get down here out of your grandmother's bedroom

14

and help me clean this bathroom before the night ends.

And just like that, it was clear to Crunchy that the time that he had just spent with his grandad was only one special dream.

So as the week drew closer to an end, back at school, the kids had been chattering and whispering about playing in the big annual Southeast Mother's Day basketball tournament.

Afraid that the kids would find it weird or strange, Crunchy kept his dream and other personal memories from this school year to himself.

On the Friday before the Mother's Day weekend, it was unclear to Mr. Leroy as to what the kids were so excited about. Although he didn't quite know what all of the hype was about, it appeared that everyone else, even Alyah, was thrilled. Everyone besides Mr.

Leroy seemed to be aware of how big of an event the basketball tournament was going to be for the community.

As Mr. Leroy made his way home on that Friday afternoon, the memory of being ignored at the end of class was still bothering him. "What in the world has gotten into my students," Mr. Leroy thought.

Mr. Leroy never listened to the radio on his commute home. But thanks to the heavy traffic, he decided to listen in hopes of maybe finding out what was causing so much congestion on the highway.

"Here we are, the station that's home to eighteen-jams in a row, the all-new hot 93.5. All of you commuters getting off of work in hopes of making it home in a hurry, we've got news from the five-o'clock traffic cam that there are delays due to construction from D.C

heading northbound to Maryland. So hold on tight and stick around for your chance to win tickets to the after-party this Saturday immediately following the youth and teen Mother's Day annual celebrity all-star basketball tournament".

Having known his class for several months now, Mr. Leroy immediately connected the dots. "My kids aren't focused on the big state test, they are all getting ready for the basketball tournament," shouted Mr. Leroy on his slow ride home.

Mr. Leroy, stuck in traffic, decided to get off of the first exit he could see. He had known that the kids all lived in different parts of the city, so finding the right neighborhood would take some effort. Mr. Leroy was, however, aware of the block that Crunchy lived in after having to write behavior referrals up for

Crunchy so many times that he memorized the address to Grandma Clara's house.

Mr. Leroy made a quick phone call home to let his family know that he would be home a little late. He plugged in the address to Crunchy's grandma's house and headed over to find him.

Unaware of Crunchy's mother's work schedule, Mr. Leroy had no idea where to start. Every other Friday, Crunchy's grandma went to visit her sister on the other side of town. Grandma Clara's sister was elderly and suffering from an illness. On these days, it usually left Crunchy's mother no choice but to ask her friend Ms. Lisa to babysit Crunchy, Nicole, and Serenity.

When Mr. Leroy arrived at Crunchy's grandma's house, there wasn't anyone anywhere in sight. Mr. Leroy parked his car, headed to the door, and knocked several times. But with the lights off and no noise coming from the inside, he just knew that he wouldn't have any luck finding him. After waiting several minutes, Mr. Leroy gave up and headed home to his own family.

The next morning was the day of the big block party and the Mother's Day Celebrity Basketball Tournament. Crunchy's mother had to work until Saturday night, which was also the night before Mother's Day. Sadly, this meant that Crunchy, Serenity, and Nicole would be stuck with Ms. Lisa and her two sons, Nasir and Cindell. Ms. Lisa's sons were twins. They were stubborn and spoiled boys who usually bragged about anything and everything.

Although they were polite to their mother and to other guests, the boys were mean and unapologetic about the way they both treated

Crunchy. The two families had been doing each other favors for years, and this weekend wasn't anything new for Crunchy and his sisters.

If Ms. Jones had to work a double or an overnight shift, her friend Ms. Lisa would watch her kids. And if Ms. Lisa needed an extra set of eyes on the boys, Grandma Jones wouldn't hesitate to put both Nasir and Cindell's irritating and disrespectful butts to work.

But on this particular weekend, a week after Crunchy had the dream that made him aware of one of his grandad's last wishes when he was alive, things seemed to only be ending with the disappointment of missing out on the basketball tournament. Instead of playing ball and participating in all of the fun, Crunchy would have to suffer at the sight of knowing that the two kids he disliked more than anyone in the world would be competing.

Even though Crunchy was finally old enough to play, his family just didn't have the $200 entry fee to sign him up for a team.

On the morning of the tournament, Nasir and Cindell woke up bragging about their new Lebron James' sneakers and how their team, the Southeast Wolves, were going to win the ten-eleven-year-old championship.

"Man...we wish you could play just so we could see the look on your face when we whoop you and your wack teammates," heckled Nasir.

"Yo...y' all lucky, this is your mom's house. Because for real...if we were at my grandma's house, I would have been knocked both of y'all out by now," replied Crunchy.

Crunchy had been working really hard on staying calm, even if someone picked on him or made him feel bad. But Nasir and Cindell were professional name-callers, and slightly bigger than Crunchy as well.

"Yeah, little Crunchy, or baby Cracky...Crummy, whatever your name is. You're lucky you aren't playing...wouldn't want to see you get beat and run home crying to your mom. Haha...that would be the worst Mother's Day gift ever. Crunchy, the crying baby," shouted Cindell.

As Ms. Lisa called for the boys, she didn't' hear the heckling that was taking place. As for Serenity and Nicole, they were usually always by Ms. Lisa's side whenever they stayed the night, so they were out of sight of all of the teasing and shouting.

Even though her sons gave Crunchy a tough time, Ms. Lisa was a nice lady and a loving person. Crunchy's sisters loved her, and they loved her back. Ms. Lisa knew that her sons were tough kids, having grown up without a father, similar to Crunchy's upbringing. But she had never suspected that they bullied Crunchy as bad as they did.

If being made fun of and preparing to miss out on playing in the tournament wasn't bad enough, Ms. Lisa had even more bad news for Crunchy.

"Hey, Charles...I have to pick up my sister and her son Damien, the superstar, who plays on the team with Nasir and Cindell. I promise if I had room in the car, I'd take you with us. But I have to get the boys to the game, and you know I can't leave your sisters here," said Ms. Lisa.

The news hit Crunchy's ears like a baseball bat smacks a ball out of the park. He couldn't believe what he was hearing. Not only was he going to miss out on actually playing, but he was being left behind like an old fried chicken bone gets left on the plate after a set of fresh hot wings comes off of the stove!

Crunchy may have been feeling sad about not being able to show off his basketball skills, but he would also be missing out on something even more dear to his heart than basketball. Alyah! Alyah's mother was an active member of the community, and she usually worked the concession stands every year at events like the Mother's Day tournament.

Crunchy had also been becoming one of Alyah's really close friends over the past few weeks, too. She managed to speak to him at the spring ice cream social, and she even complimented him on his poem that he wrote in April.

But Ms. Lisa didn't know, nor would she care about that. Her concern as a mother was getting her sons to the game and keeping her house organized.

"Oh, and one more thing," added Ms. Lisa. While I'm gone, can you do me a favor please and clean up the kitchen after you and the boys were in there eating and making a mess," asked Ms. Lisa

Crunchy took a deep breath and exhaled slowly. "Okay…" sadly replied Crunchy.

Before the boys exited the house to join their mother and Crunchy's sisters in the car, the two of them knocked over the trash can and spilled milk onto the kitchen table to make Crunchy's job even more difficult.

"Yo, man," hollered out Crunchy.

The boys ran out the front door, jumped into the car, let out their last laughs, and with their heads sticking out of the windows, chuckled from ear to ear.

Back inside of the kitchen, Crunchy was at a loss for words. He had been sad all week leading up to Mother's Day weekend for so many reasons. His mind bounced around from being unsure if he was going to be prepared to do well on the big state tests and then back to whether or not Ms. Lisa would change her mind and come back for him so that he could at least enjoy watching the tournament.

Just as Crunchy went to stand the milk carton back up, there he was. Standing again before Crunchy was Granda Jones.

"Haha...man, this is crazy...you're back," happily jumped and shouted out Crunchy.

"I'm always with you when you need me, Charles, but I don't have a lot of time. I came to bring you these sneakers that you are going to use for the tournament today," called out Grandad Jones. "These are special sneakers that

26

will provide you with the skills you need to be the greatest basketball player that you can be."

Crunchy didn't want to tell his grandad the bad news, but he figured that it wouldn't be right if he kept his thoughts to himself.

"Well, I won't be playing ball today, grandad," sighed Crunchy.

"We didn't have enough money to put a team together, and to make things worse, I don't even have a ride to go watch the teams play."

Then without warning, Crunchy heard not one, not two, but three familiar voices shouting from outside of the front of Lisa's house.

CHAPTER THREE

Just as he did about a week ago during breakfast at his grandma's house, Grandad Jones had disappeared on Crunchy and was now gone again.

At that moment, running up to greet Crunchy at the door of Ms. Lisa's house was a group that Crunchy would have never ever expected to see. Coming to Crunchy's rescue

28

was Jamal, Kelvin, Mr. Leroy, and some of Crunchy's best friends from his neighborhood.

"Man...I know you wasn't over here sweepin' and cleanin' up after Nas and Dell ole' crazy butts," said Kelvin.

"My mom, man. She works until later today, so Ms. Lisa was baby sittin' us," replied Crunchy.

"But yo, are y'all here to save me," asked Crunchy.

Crunchy, still holding the broom in his hand that he was going to use to clean up the mess in the kitchen that he didn't even make, was now standing in front of his two classmates and their teacher, Mr. Leroy.

"Man...you'll never guess what's goin' on right now", said Jamal. "Mr. Leroy heard about the basketball tournament. He drove all around D.C like a crazy Uber driver, scooped us all up, signed us all up, and now he's gonna coach us today at the b-ball tournament," finished Jamal as he excitedly explained what was happening.

"Wait...yooo....that's crazy," replied Crunchy.

Mr. Leroy thought that now would be a good time to jump in. "So what's up, Charles...I mean, *Crunchy*. My squad could use a big man. I already asked your grandmother, and she was letting your mother know that you'd be on my team as we were driving over here to get you. What do you say," asked an excited Mr. Leroy.

Crunchy didn't hesitate to join the guys. He threw down the broom, grabbed the sneakers that he had received by *Grandad Jones*, and was out of the door as fast as lightning!

As the team drove over to the basketball park, they arrived just in time to register. As they finished signing up, they waited for Mr. Leroy's next direction. As the boys waited to figure out where to prepare for their first game, they watched Nasir, Cindell, and their cousin Damien, the AAU travel team player of the year, walk by.

"Man...guys, that's Damien. He's the best player out here," nervously mentioned Crunchy. "Nobody can stop him."

Mr. Leroy had been a star athlete for as far back as he could remember, years and years before ever becoming an NFL superstar. So he knew first-hand what fear sounded like coming from a kid.

So at that moment, he knew that he would have to do something to calm Crunchy's nerves.

For the past three years, Damien had been known by everyone in the city as the next Kevin Durant. That would be an almost perfect description of Damien, except last year during his tenth birthday party, he had the chance to play KD one on one, and he beat him. Damien...beat Kevin Durant. And he beat him so bad that the NBA almost traded him for Damien except for the fact that Damien was only in the 6th grade; not quite old enough to sign an NBA contract.

But just as the tournament got underway, Mr. Leroy's team, who decided to call themselves the Elite All-Stars, managed to win their first three games.

Game one for the Elite All-Stars was close. Crunchy scored eight points but had a bad attitude when things didn't seem to be going his way.

Crunchy's team dominated in game two, but Mr. Leroy had to sit Crunchy out a couple of times to calm him down after arguing with a kid from the other team.

And even though they won game three, they did so with Crunchy mainly on the bench, sitting side by side Mr. Leroy as Mr. Leroy tried encouraging Crunchy to be more of a team player.

"Charles, you're a good player, but the best players cheer their teammates on," shared Mr. Leroy during the end of the first three games.

During the early rounds of the tournament, Crunchy, who was great at scoring but who was not so great on defense, allowed his poor attitude to get to him. When kids on the other teams scored against his teammates, instead of playing smart and encouraging his teammates, he'd catch an attitude and make careless mistakes, taking the role of a poor sport.

Although the boys had won all of their games, placing them in the finals for their age group, Mr. Leroy had no choice but to sit

Crunchy for a quarter in hopes of teaching him how to be accountable for his actions.

Mr. Leroy, sure that Crunchy would be upset for a while, leaned down to whisper to Crunchy.

"Charles, between you and I, I know you've got it in you to lead by example out there on the court. When you get your chance to do so, make your family proud," added Mr. Leroy.

"Hey, Mr. Leroy, I know Crunchy let his anger get to him in the first couple of games, but we need him to score if we are going to win against the best team in the tournament," suggested Jamal.

Mr. Leroy went on to explain to the guys that sometimes, sports are not all about winning.

"As of matter of fact, guys, tell me this...how do you feel about the *school year* this far," asked Mr. Leroy.

The looks on the guys' faces were a sure sign that Mr. Leroy brought up a topic that they hadn't planned on talking about during a basketball tournament. But without hesitation, Crunchy began to answer. "You were kind of like a father to me this year in school, Mr. Leroy. And not having a dad to help me with stuff, it kind of feels like...like I have one at school. In October, it was rough, but now it kind of feels good because I used to be off-task and get into a lot of trouble. But when I see you every day, I want to make better choices."

Out of nowhere, Jamal spoke up. "And you didn't get in a lot of suspensions like you did last year, Crunchy. And...we didn't know how to be successful or well...what being successful looked like until now. But if we are gonna win this game, we need Crunchy out there," added Jamal.

"Jamal, I understand that you want to win, but I need to make sure you boys are learning what it means to have sportsmanship and respect," explained Mr. Leroy.

The news spread from one side of the park to the other that in the opposite bracket, the Southeast Wolves were sending other teams home crying to their moms, embarrassed that they even showed up to play the Wolves. The Wolves finished their first three games undefeated, as well.

As the tournament was only one game away from crowning a winner, the Elite All-Stars were set to face the Southeast Wolves in the championship round.

Although Nasir, Cindell, and Damien were

playing in the Mother's Day tournament for the first time, it wasn't their first time playing on the same team together. The boys had chemistry together. Ever since they were all six and seven-years-old, their moms had them practicing and playing on the same team.

Crunchy and his classmates were great athletes, but the city was sure that no other group of kids were any match for the Southeast Wolves.

"Alright party people, we are getting ready for the youth championship match between the ferocious Southeast Wolves," shouted out the MC of the tournament.

Based on the energy that the crowd gave off with the announcement, it appeared that the Wolves were going to be the hometown favorite as the crowd erupted with cheers when Damien waved and interacted with the crowd of about two-hundred spectators.

"The Wolves will be playing against a team with some fresh faces and some new talent, coached by the one and only Tyron Leroy...let's give it up for the Elite All-Stars," hollered out the commentator.

The wolves were obviously the crowd favorite as Crunchy's team only seemed to get some cheers and praises that sounded more like applause for Mr. Leroy. There were only four or five faces in the crowd that seemed to be excited to cheer them on.

As the game got ready to start, Mr. Leroy called his boys over for one final pep-talk.

"Hey...no reason to be nervous. We did great for the first few games. We are winners. No matter what happens, I'm proud of you boys. Teamwork on three. One. Two. Three. Teamwork" hollered Mr. Leroy's team.

"Oh, hey...Charles" shouted Mr. Leroy. "Don't worry if we get behind early on...I heard that these boys score a lot in the beginning and get tired towards the end. But that's fine. Remember this--Every point counts."

CHAPTER FOUR

As the game began, it started off just as Mr. Leroy predicted. At the end of the first quarter, the Wolves were ahead of the All-Stars by ten points.

Crunchy's cousin, Rae'Anna, had been studying on campus for a May final exam but was able to convince two of her roommates to come out and support her cousin Lil' Crunchy at the game.

"Yo, Yo, Yo...little cuz...you got this," shouted Rae'Anna from the stands.

As the All-Stars huddled up before the start of the second quarter, Mr. Leroy attempted to make some changes to give them a better chance at winning. "Okay boys, we are doing alright. But talk to me, what's happening out there," asked Mr. Leroy.

"I can't stop Damien," said one of Crunchy's teammates.

So for the second quarter, Mr. Leroy put Jamal in charge of stopping Damien.

"Man, you can't stop me either," called out Damien as he noticed the switch.

Damien got the ball at the top of the three-point line and made one stutter-step move to get Jamal off balance. Damien zoomed past Jamal as if Jamal was made out of a few pieces of straw. Damien was too much for Jamal to handle, blowing past him for one easy lay-up after another.

By the end of the second quarter, it was evident that the boys were going to have to make another change to their game plan if they expected to win.

As the third quarter got underway, Crunchy and his teammates were still only behind by ten points. It seemed that Crunchy was a tough player for the Wolves to guard as well. So with another attempt at stopping Damien from scoring, Kelvin was now in charge of defending him.

"Ut, oh, looks like I have another weak challenge in front of me. You guys can't stop me," chuckled Damien.

Damien got the ball at the top of the three-point line, made one stutter-step move and crossed over on Kelvin to get a clear path to the hoop. Damien brushed by Kelvin as if Kelvin was made out of a few pieces of stick, loosely bound together, unable to hold Damien back from ballin' out as he continued to score one easy lay-up after another.

By the end of the third quarter, it was apparent that the boys were going to have to make one more change to their game plan if they were going to come back.

As the fourth quarter got underway, Crunchy and his teammates were now only four points behind the Wolves. Crunchy was proving to be a great competitor as he was outscoring both Jamal and Kelvin and was also managing to play a little tougher on defense than the other boys on his team.

So with perhaps their last attempt at stopping Damien from scoring, Mr. Leroy looked over onto the court and gave Crunchy a look that he had never shown the boys before. It was a mean look, an urgent stare...but one of super-competitive nature.

At that moment, Crunchy read Mr. Leroy's body language and understood his facial expressions. Crunchy knew that it was his turn to try to defend Damien.

With only one minute left in the game, Damien inbounded the ball and dribbled it up the court. The Wolves were still in the lead, but just by two points.

Damien passed the ball to Nasir, who was looking to take a shot. Nasir was stopped by Jamal and forced to pass the ball back to Damien. Damien now had the ball at the top of the three-point line, which was his favorite spot on the court. With time winding down, he made one stutter-step move, crossed over dribbled to get a clear path to the hoop, but Crunchy, standing his ground like a chunk of bricks, took one strong step to his right and stopped Damien who was trying to blow past him. Crunchy, still playing terrific defense, got back in perfect position, waited for Damien to try his stutter-step move a second time, and with perfect timing, knocked the ball from Damien's handle.

Crunchy, racing for the ball as it was now bouncing in the direction of their basket, grabbed the loose ball and passed it to Jamal, who was open for a three-pointer.

But Cindell, hustling back to play defense, jumped in front of Jamal, forcing Jamal to look for another open player. Jamal spotted Kelvin, who was standing directly behind the three-point line. With all of the strength that he had left, Jamal passed the ball to Kelvin, who, with three seconds left in the game, set up to shoot what would be the game-winning basket.

With his last efforts at winning the game, Kelvin shot what seemed to be the potential buzzer-beating, game-winning shot.

The ball was now in the air. It was rotating perfectly and twirling in the direction of the rim. The boys' PE teacher Mr. Williams, their school counselor Mrs. Moniz and the principal Mrs. Morris, who had been cheering on the All-Stars all day, were now standing tall on their feet. This seemed like the perfect moment in the making that everyone would be proud of the boys for.

What felt like days, was only seconds. The ball seemed suspended in the air as the staff members shouted and yelled out loud the words, "go in...go...in…go...in," causing the phrase to stretch across the entire park in slow motion.

The ball hit the side of the rim, rattled around the perfect circle for two full rotations, in and out, in and out, as it finally swirled a third time before tipping over and falling on the *outside* of the rim. The ball, dropping to the ground in super slow motion, meant that the game was now over.

And just like that, Crunchy's dream of bringing the Mother's Day championship home was over. The Wolves had beaten the All-Stars by two points.

But what the Wolves had not anticipated was how the crowd would react as they screamed in excitement, jumping up and down as the winning team.

CHAPTER FIVE

Sometimes in life, winning actually isn't *everything*. Sometimes, how you win is just as important as or even more important than the final score of a game.

The Wolves had won the championship. There was no doubt that they were talented athletes. But what people had unfortunately noticed even more than the fact that they won was their negative attitudes throughout the tournament.

The Southeast Wolves had talked junk during every game, and people had heard how they treated the All-Stars on the court. They were ferocious competitors, but they pushed and fouled players with unnecessary force whenever a kid from another team dared to try scoring on them.

The only thing that the crowd had seen or heard from the All-Stars during the game was how well and how hard they worked as a team to try their best and never give up.

As the afternoon settled down, and Mr. Leroy prepared to get all of the boys back home, he reminded Crunchy and the guys one more time of how proud of them he was.

"Man, guys...you have no reason to feel bad

about losing. You gave it your all and never quit on each other. That...is all that truly matters right now. In sports and in life, every point can change the outcome of the game. And *we* were so close to winning. So use this as a lesson for next time you face a challenge."

That night, Crunchy's mom wanted to hear all about the games and how much fun he had while playing in his first basketball tournament. But with every passing moment, Crunchy couldn't help but think about his grandad.

He wondered if his grandad would be proud of him for playing hard and never giving up. He thought about if his grandad had been alive to see him play, would he have been proud of Crunchy for showing persistence by not shutting down even when Mr. Leroy didn't let him play.

He wondered if he would have made his

grandad proud by the way he acted when things weren't going his way. He thought about how bad he wanted nothing more than to make people proud by being a winner.

But then Crunchy began to think a bit more negatively. He wondered if his grandad would be disappointed because of how the boys came so close to winning the championship but eventually fell short. He wondered if he would ever see his grandad again and if he was the only one in the family that thought about his grandad so much.

"Hey, sorry, mom...I know you wanna know about the game and all, but we lost in the championship to Ms. Lisa's kids," said Crunchy.

"Aww, it's okay, Crunchy. I heard from someone special, who was there watching you play the whole time that you would have made me so proud. It doesn't matter that you didn't win the championship," said Crunchy's mom. "What matters the most is that you played hard, you never gave up, and you used your second chance to lead by example."

Crunchy was confused. He knew that his mom may have been able to text Ms. Lisa or ask someone from the neighborhood how the boys ended up doing overall. But how was it possible that she knew about the encouraging and inspiring words that Mr. Leroy shared with Crunchy? Maybe Mr. Leroy called her and shared the news of their successful day.

As the ladies, Crunchy's mom, his grandma, and aunt worked in the house cooking and preparing food for tomorrow's Mother's Day feast, Crunchy couldn't help but think about who his mom was referring to. Who was the "someone special" who told her about his goal of *leading by example*?

The ladies continued to cook, laugh, and reminisce with one another in the kitchen as the kids all hung out in the living room that Saturday night.

"Oh, girls...I sure do miss *that man*," sighed Grandma Jones from the kitchen.

It wouldn't be a D.C spring if people weren't still excited and playin' in that ole' Mother's Day basketball tournament that the Boys and Girls club been putting on since way back in the ole' Chuck Brown Go-Go Days. Mmmhmmm...Those was the days...Trouble Funk Band and all of the good stuff used to play at those block parties. I remember taking y'all down there to watch my husband play and win that city championship each and every Mother's Day. When I met Noah, he was winning those games for his own mother. Then, we ended up being together so long that he even won the championship a couple of times after I had you," called out Grandma Jones to Crunchy's mom.

"Mom, I can't believe that man of yours been involved in that event for what...twenty-five, thirty-years," asked Crunchy's mom.

Grandma Jones replied, "Crunchy's grandad was one of the most important members of the community since as far back as I could remember. He usually organized the basketball tournament. He used to sign up and pay for boys whose daddies couldn't afford to pay for them, and he even made sure everyone had enough food to eat."

"You're forgetting one thing," said Crunchy's mom as she turned on the kitchen radio. "My daddy also remembered to find a DJ to make sure that we all had some music to dance to after them basketball game was all over."

"I know that's right, excitedly added Grandma Jones.

The ladies danced the night away as Crunchy, and the kids all fell asleep in the living room, watching one of their favorite movies.

The very next morning was Mother's Day. There was no announcement needed as the house had a warm, loving scent seeping from the kitchen, entering every single room until it reached the living room where Crunchy, his sisters, and cousins had all fallen asleep.

Yawning and awakening from the aroma, Crunchy's eyes popped open like a kid on Christmas Day.

"Oh my goodness, it smells bangin' in there....smells like someone came down from

Heaven and cooked breakfast, lunch and all the best desserts in the world," called out Crunchy.

As Grandma Jones walked into the living room to wake all of the kids, one by one, they all sprung up like grasshoppers and gave their grandma big ole' hugs. "Happy Mother's Day," shouted the kids.

"Thank you, thank you, my lovely, beautiful chocolate grandbabies," replied Grandma Jones.

The family took the next hour or so to take showers, to get dressed, and to prepare themselves for what was already a very special day. As the family took turns eating and handing their Mother's Day cards out, it seemed as if something was missing.

Crunchy, Serenity, and Nicole gave their mother a card, their grandma a card, and their aunt a card. Crunchy's cousins did the same,

56

making sure every special woman in the kids' lives were aware of how much the kids appreciated all three of their queens.

But as the afternoon began to come to a close, something remained unsettling inside the house. Crunchy overhead, his mother and grandma talking as the rest of the kids watched TV and sang songs in the living room.

"I know that he used nutmeg, cinnamon, and a little bit of honey. But God, how I wish I knew what that last ingredient was to make these pies taste exactly like how daddy used to make them," cried out Crunchy's mom.

"I know, baby. It'll be okay. We can start a new tradition with a different kind of dessert," replied Grandma Jones.

Crunchy knew that when grown-ups were talking that he wasn't supposed to interrupt them or join in on the conversation. But something deep down in his soul made him feel that in that exact moment, it was more than okay to do so but that adding himself to the conversation was the right thing to do.

"Three tablespoons of brown sugar should be added to each pie. Yeah...that's what's missing," boldly called out Crunchy.

Crunchy's grandma heard where the suggestion was coming from, blinked her eyes about a million times before the memory of her late husband came flooding back to her.

Mrs. Jones, standing in the kitchen in front of Crunchy and her daughter, was speechless. She hadn't heard the phrase, "three tablespoons of brown sugar should be added to each pie" in over six years.

Somewhere lost and buried away with the fact that she lost her husband too soon and that the kids had lost their only grandad too early, was also any of the memorable times that she and Noah had spent with one another cooking and baking their favorite dishes.

"Three tablespoons of brown sugar should be added to each pie," resounded in Grandma Jones' head as tears also formed in the wells of her eyes.

And just as if Mr. Noah Jones himself were there cooking with the family in the kitchen, Crunchy's mother offered him a spoon and the container of brown sugar, giving Crunchy the okay to add the final ingredients into all five of the pies that the ladies had prepared.

As the pies finished baking, the family finished their Mother's Day feast with the best present that anyone could have ever wished for.

CHAPTER SIX

On the other side of town, Mr. Leroy and his family members were having a unique Mother's Day experience of their own.

"Girls--," called Mr. Leroy to his two daughters. "Mommy is going to love both of your cards the same," said Mr. Leroy as he tried calming his two angry daughters down.

Mr. Leroy's daughters were having a hard

60

time treating each other nicely after his youngest daughter said that her Mother's Day card, which she made, was better than the one her sister made.

It was clear that whenever Mr. Leroy's daughters disagreed with one another that it upset him. He was a man of love, unity, and family. So arguing instead of supporting one another wasn't the best thing to do in front of Mr. Leroy

"Okay, girls," sternly said, Mr. Leroy. "I'll tell you what. When mommy comes downstairs, we will let her decide whose card is better," suggested Mr. Leroy.

Tyron Leroy had known his wife for ten years, and if he knew anything about her at all, it was that she was full of kindness and love. As the girls ran over to their mommy shouting out, "read mine, read mine, read mine," their mother

Mrs. Leroy grabbed both cards at the same time, shouted out, thank you, and gave her two daughters great big hugs and kisses on the forehead.

"Ahem," sounded Mr. Leroy as he batted his eyebrows at his wife, indicating that the girls were having a disagreement.

"Mommy, tell me that my card is the best," cried out Mr. Leroy's youngest daughter.

"No, mommy, tell me that my card is soo much better," called out Mr. Leroy's firstborn.

Mr. Leroy, standing about a million feet higher than where the girls were now on their knees cuddled next to their kneeling mother, tried his hardest not to laugh, already knowing the answer to the questions.

"Well, this is not a difficult question or job to do at all," replied Mrs. Leroy. "Why I think both of these Mother's Day cards are the most beautiful cards in the whole wide world. They are both going to hang up in mommy's room, right next to my favorite picture of daddy."

So once the Mother's Day cards were received and the girls got their answer, the four of them, Mr. Leroy, his wife, and their two daughters, all joined in for a huge Leroy family group hug.

CHAPTER SEVEN

That evening, Mr. Leroy had kissed his daughters good night. He then made sure that his wife's day went well. Finally, he said his prayers for protection over his family as well as for all of his students. He knew that the kids would be taking the big state test the very next day, so he wanted to send up a special prayer for them.

That next morning in school, although the Elite All-Stars had lost to the Southeast Wolves, Crunchy, Jamal, and Kelvin were once again friends. All year, the guys had been treating each other like pals one day and then bullying each other around the next. But today, during breakfast in class and on the first day of state testing, they were back to being *tight* again.

"Good morning Crunchy, I saw your hard work and concentration pay off at the tournament," said Alyah.

Although Crunchy had spoken to Alyah a few times this year, hearing her voice was still the most exciting part of his day. After her comment, he immediately began to daydream. "Oooh, Alyah...how I adore my beautiful, smart, kind and lov---"

"Man...If you don't snap out of that love spell that Alyah put you under," shouted Kelvin as he had noticed Crunchy lose focus. "We have test number one today for reading. I can't have my boy daydreaming about holding hands and sharing ice cream sundaes. We gotta get you ready for middle school, bruh."

As Crunchy, Jamal, and Kelvin laughed with each other, Mr. Leroy was making sure that everyone had thrown away their trash before beginning their first major test. The time was now 8:30 am, and it was officially time to start.

Mr. Leroy passed out chrome books to every student in the class as they were all instructed to sit silently until he provided them with their username testing tickets, passwords, and final instructions.

"Good morning class, today you will take

the first section of the English Language Arts test. You may now open your Chromebooks, login, and click next. Follow along as I read the directions on the screen.

Crunchy couldn't help but be nervous on the day of testing. He had known for sure that he was going to be able to get some questions right. But he was also convinced that there would be some questions where he would lose points.

He began to think about how many points he would receive for a reading comprehension question. He began to think about how much each written response section was worth. He was afraid that after all of the days in class this year, that he wouldn't have the skills down to get a passing score.

Mr. Leroy continued. "You will have ninety-minutes to complete section one of the

ELA test. I will not be able to help you answer any test questions, so make sure you read every passage and reread each question if you are confused. When you are finished, I will collect your testing material, and you will sit silently until the time has ended. Oh, and one more thing…forget all of the drama and stress from any challenging situations that took place this school year. Each and every one of you will do great. You may now begin the test and remember that...every point counts."

Special words from the author

WE BELIEVE IN YOU, BUT DO YOU BELIEVE IN YOU?

So...hopefully by now, it is clear that we teachers and adults who care about all of you students and young people so much were once elementary, middle, and high school students ourselves. And what that means is that we know what it is like to struggle to believe.

We know exactly what it feels like to sit in class and have to learn about something that may not seem too appealing right away. We know exactly why all of a sudden, you ask to use the bathroom when you either see or hear your best friend from another class head in that direction.

So believe us when we tell you that we know how smart and creative you all can be when you put your minds to it. Instead of finding excuses for why you don't have the **confidence** in yourself, know that as soon as you make a choice to try, trying becomes a habit. Take, for example, one student from my past teaching experience.

One day a few years ago, I had sat down with one of my favorite students. Those moments of being able to converse without direct instruction are always a fun time. I had never known how to relate to each individual struggle or how to understand where each child was coming from regarding how they viewed themselves as a student, a son, or as a daughter. Each scholar in my classroom had a unique story, and each experience was always worth hearing.

Talking to one of my 4th graders at the end of the school year a few years ago had been a very fascinating experience. She came to my class in August of 2014 with the excitement and energy that you would love to see in every child in America. But what I immediately found out about her was that she was going to teach me way more than she was going to learn from me.

Yes…was the first word she said to me when I asked her to tell me about her year in the fourth grade.

"It was fun, having to learn more of having what I had learned in third grade and to be in Yale (the name of our classroom) and to have you, Mr. Mourning, as my teachers."

I asked her about how hard she thought everything was for her after having gone to summer school last year, where I had the pleasure of teaching her for a full month of additional instruction before starting fourth grade.

She responded by telling me that fourth grade was hard because there were things that she couldn't do but that she learned how to do them by paying attention. She continued to explain how she was confused as to why the teachers were always redirecting her and that she thought we didn't like her. That was until she went home one afternoon, and her mom told her that I had called her to explain how proud I had been that she worked through being upset as she often became emotional with challenging activities and tasks.

The most challenging scenario with this one student was breaking down her barriers that she obviously learned to use to avoid tasks and to get out of doing work that would push her to her limits. I could only imagine what being asked to read grade-level texts and to complete written assignments designed for students equipped with the skillset most educators would deem as proficient for grade-level expectations would feel like for an entire year if you had, in fact, not been prepared to do so. I clearly had to differentiate and scaffold tasks and activities for this particular student, but what is more important in this case was her willingness to continue trying once her frustration and self-doubting episodes would pass.

She grew to love her classmates and learned that education was not just something that adults talked about. But instead, she learned that if she believed in herself long enough that she could accomplish most of what we asked of her. It is safe to say that though she will continue to be challenged throughout her formal educational journey, she will at least know the importance of giving it her best shot, no matter what obstacles are in front of her.

For those of you who are afraid of trying because you aren't sure if you will be able to make other people around you proud, remember that you don't have to prove yourself to anyone. Instead of worrying about proving people wrong who may not believe in you, focus more on proving yourself right.

The goals and things you want to accomplish are going to help you out in life, so don't worry about what others think while you are on your way to the top. Do not get into the habit of listening to anything negative people have to say about your efforts or abilities to accomplish goals or tasks.

Be sure to focus on yourself and on the effort that you give when it comes to believing you can achieve. That way, anything that isn't positive or supportive that people have to say about you won't matter at all.

Had I let what kids said about me stop me from believing in myself when I was younger, I would have never been able to make anything out of myself.

If I had let growing up without a father and without fresh new clothes, stop me from trying my hardest and caring about my school work, my life would have gone down the *wrong* path.

Instead, listen to adults when they tell you they want to *help* you and that regardless of what your life is like now, you have all of the ability you need. All of the tools to become someone and something great right now or very soon are already in your hands. All you have to do is figure out how to use them.

Let's stop for a second and imagine this...Pretend that you fall overboard off of a massive boat in the middle of an ocean. In that instance, huge waves would come crashing down on you, making it hard to survive. But the waves aren't the only thing that can harm you. There are also sharks! Big ones, too! But if someone threw over a life raft to save you, what would you do?

If you ignore your teachers and disrespect the adults who care about you and don't take us seriously when we tell you that you can "do it", it is the same as ignoring the life raft that was thrown overboard to save your life.

Instead of being pulled up to safety, you would be left stranded in the ocean with those life-threatening waves. Oh, and the sharks. Can't forget about the sharks. Instead of accepting the support and making "trying your hardest," a new habit, you would be letting yourself sink deeper and deeper into the ocean, never reaching land again.

The same way those people using that life raft would be trained to properly bring you to safety is the same way your teachers are trained in caring for you.

Your teachers are trained to make sure you are ready for the challenges of hard school work. Your parents and other adults are experienced enough to point you in the right direction during a challenging time in your life. They are also trained to make sure that when you get to the next grade or turn another year older, that you are confident in yourselves. We are prepared to make sure that you believe you can be successful at whatever it is that you have to do.

But that isn't enough! The point of this book is to show you that, of course, we care about you and that we believe in you. However, you have to believe in yourself even more than we do and **interpret** these **skills** in a way that you can use them throughout your life and **recall** them when necessary.

How many of you have ever said, "I can't do it". At some point, we all say things like that. It is because, for a moment, we forget to believe in ourselves. It is because, in those true moments of feeling **inadequate**, we feel that we can **justify** or explain giving up on ourselves.

When things get hard or scary, feeling like quitting and backing away from something hard is what we think to do. It's natural…I get it. But instead of feeling that way, know that somebody out there who cares about you more than they care about anything in the world believes that you can do whatever you put your mind to.

A Special Thank you...

On a cold October afternoon, my stomach was twisting and turning with anxiety. I was only ten years old, and yet, I had been exposed to more opportunities to assume adult-like responsibilities than most twenty-year-olds are given. I was often responsible for making sure my two siblings and I, at the time, made it to school before 7:45 a.m. every morning. I was more often than not the person checking to make sure the three of us had clean clothes for the next day and that our homework was done the night before school. And more importantly, to mention, I was responsible for keeping us safe.

On that winter-like afternoon back in 1997, I was living the life of being one of the top youth football players in my town for the past two years. As a young athlete, football was one of the only things in my life that I seemed to have success with. Therefore, the opportunity of achieving my goal at one day becoming a professional football player was what I held onto the most. I was determined and had all of the intentions in the world on keeping that momentum for myself going.

Although I had the potential for being a young superstar in the making, one thing was determined to keep me from achieving my goals. Throughout my childhood, my mother didn't have a car. This often caused my siblings and I to miss out on several extracurricular opportunities. From our school to the playing fields, I could remember everything being very far away and out of walking distance.

Missing practices and making excuses for not being able to participate in activities several miles away from my home would have been understandable. But as life would go on, I came to find out that by not allowing obstacles to stop me from maximizing my chances to achieve great things, and by never giving up hope even when things aren't going my way, that at some point a window of opportunity will come by.

So on that cold, damp afternoon in October of 1997, as a ten-year-old football player and big brother, I walked for five miles to practice with my youth football team that day. And about one hundred feet from the parking lot, I was approached by a car. Driving was the father of a family whose son played on my team, and they asked me how long I had been walking. And what I remember telling them was that I didn't know for sure, but I knew that I didn't want to miss my opportunity to be the best football player in town this season. As chance has it, and commonly for many families around the country, I became the kid who the Weiss Family always picked up and brought home from practice.

From that day on, I saw the power in taking action. I chose to be accountable and to never use excuses for the lack of opportunities to improve my life. Instead, I realized that by showing effort and trying your hardest to get the job done, that it would always maximize my chances at a positive future for my own life.

By identifying open windows of opportunity, it is never too late to find a way out of no way. My mother was only two more practices away from pulling me off of that team because of her not knowing how she was going to provide safe and adequate transportation for her first son. But perhaps walking, as safe of a route as I knew, I somehow showed my dedication and passion to the world, which changed the trajectory of my life for the better. And in 2009, after completing four years of college, receiving two degrees and participating as a full-scholarship athlete, I thank those who stopped along the road who offered me a ride. Life...what a ride it will be.

ABOUT THE AUTHOR

Glen Leroy Mourning was born on March 26th, 1987, in Danbury, Connecticut. As the oldest of his mother Lillian's five children, Glen was blessed with the opportunity to lead by example where he would become the first of two generations to not only graduate from high school but to complete a Master's Degree.

In 2005 Glen earned a Full- Athletic Scholarship to attend the University of Connecticut, where he would make the All-Big East Conference Academic Honor roll for two years in a row before graduating and attending Grad School at the University of Bridgeport. In 2010 Glen finished his Master's Degree in Elementary Ed. and was named the student-teacher of the year at the University of Bridgeport. Since then, Glen worked alongside of the nationally renowned Educational contributor Dr. Steve Perry, Star of the CNN Special "Black in America II" and the host of TV One's "Save our Sons".

As a 4th and 5th grade teacher at Capital Preparatory Magnet School in Hartford, Connecticut, Glen managed to brilliantly inspire the lives of hundreds of students in his tenure as an educator. At the same time, he was the assistant varsity football coach at Capital Prep, where the team posted an incredible record of 22-2, winning State playoff appearances before stepping down from his role as the defensive backs coach.

For the past year, Glen has worked in Washington D.C as a 4th grade teacher. Glen and his wife Nicole will continue working together in education in Washington, D.C., where they hope to continue writing and sharing literature for young people in America.

Glen's most significant accomplishments are not those that have occurred on the playing fields across America but rather with his promise to his family that he has kept, which was to become the motivation for his students that have come from similar circumstances.

More from the Author

Crunchy Life Book 1: Recess Detention

In book 1 of the Crunchy Life Series, students are challenged
to think about what challenges they face on a daily basis that
may distract them from being the best that they can be.
Students often face problems that can easily overwhelm
them, but what may also be hard for a kid to communicate to
adults. Keep track of how Crunchy attempts to make smart
choices in a confusing and challenging world. When times are
tough, be sure to find positive people to surround yourself
with.

Crunchy Life Book 2: Naughty or Nice for the Holidays

In book 2 of the Crunchy Life Series, students are challenged to think about times where they have had to serve a consequence after making a poor choice. Students often struggle with feeling as if they are bad kids. But in reality, sometimes kids simply make "bad" choices. Keep track of how Crunchy responds to his challenges. Always make good choices to avoid being naughty.

Crunchy Life Book 3: Tough Cookies

In book 3 of the Crunchy Life Series, students are challenged to have an open mind and hear from multiple perspectives. Students often struggle with learning new information, especially if it goes against what adults tell them. Keep track of how Crunchy grows as a thinker, as well as how he builds his confidence. Always be willing to learn new things!

Crunchy Life Book 4: One Piece at a Time

In book 4 of the Crunchy Life Series, students are challenged to differentiate between huge life problems and smaller problems that can be handled with coping skills. Students often struggle with thinking that no one understands how they feel. The truth is, adults want students to learn how to persevere. Keep track of how Crunchy pushes through tough situations. Always accept responsibility for your own actions.

Care More Than Us: The Young People's Guide to Success and student work book.

"Care More Than Us" is a conversation style read for young readers and teenagers alike, who may have trouble identifying how great they or their students and children already are. By readjusting what it means to be successful, "Care More Than Us" takes the readers through the process of learning to believe in themselves and avoiding the crowd that may distract them from reaching their goals. This guide to success will allow students to see that by caring more than adults do about their own futures, that they will be able to build a world where accomplishing goals is their main priority. Young people will read about what it means to become accountable for their actions, along with why never giving up will help them build life-long habits. Finally, readers will be able to refer back to the steps of achieving success where they will ultimately learn to love school and learning, over and over again. The tools for a successful journey are finally here! Learn how to care enough to change your life one day at a time.

<u>Strategies to positively handle "crunchy" situations.</u>

When life seems challenging and things aren't going your way, remember that if you stay positive and calm that you will be alright.

1. **Ask yourself why you're angry (problem solve).** If you ask yourself why you're angry, and really think about your answer, you might figure out a problem you can solve or even uncover some of the sneaky feelings that feel like anger.

2. **Use "if-then" statements to consider the consequences.** If-then statements mean that you ask yourself what might happen if you do something. They are best used when you are deciding what to do about a situation or problem. If-then statements help you make better choices by helping you understand the consequences of your actions.

3. **Count up to or down from 10.** Sometimes, quietly counting to 10 is something some people do to stop themselves from doing something too quickly. Counting to 10 as soon as you notice you're having an angry reaction can give an angry person just enough think time to make sure their first idea is a good idea. If it's not a good idea, it can be just enough time to change it into a better one (reconsider).

4. **Listen to another person.** If you're angry about something or with someone else, talking to someone and listening to their perspective—even the person you're angry with—may help you understand exactly what caused the problem so you can fix it or figure out what you can do in the future to prevent the situation.

5. **Focus on your breathing.** Focusing on breathing can help during angry moments in several ways. First, it takes your attention away from the anger for a moment, just like when you count to 10. Second, breathing in a certain way, slowly and deeply (so deeply that your belly moves, too), and in through your nose and out through your mouth, can often help people who are angry to begin to calm down.

6. **Take a walk or step away.** Change the environment by taking a walk or stepping away if you can. Just like counting to 10, and thinking about your breathing, walking away from a situation that is making you angry can sometimes help prevent you from reacting to a situation too quickly, or it can give you some time to breathe and think about good choices you can make.

7. **Give yourself some good advice (self-talk).** Self-talk means that you say to yourself the things that a good friend would say to calm you down, such as, "Calm down," "Maybe it's not that bad," or "Let it go." It is best used when you first notice that you are angry (emotional reaction stage). Its purpose is to help calm you down. Use self-talk if you notice yourself using any thinking errors (use logic).

8. **Look for the humor—without making fun of someone.** Sometimes we get angry for silly reasons that are hard to explain. Maybe you don't even really want to be angry. Sometimes, if there is no danger, you can count to 10 and imagine what it must look like if this whole angry situation was something you were watching in a TV comedy. Sometimes, when you really think about it, some of the things that make us angry can seem really silly. Remember, though, that if you are involved in an angry situation with someone else, they may not think it's funny at the same time you do. It usually works best if you can laugh at yourself.

Source: https://blog.brookespublishing.com/8-anger-management-tips-for-your-students/

To submit your questions about Crunchy Life or on learning strategies on how to deal with challenging situations, email mourningknows@gmail.com

Submit your Crunchy Conversation Testimonials to mourningknows@gmail.com and share with author Glen Mourning how you faced a challenging situation and how you were able to persevere.

For more information, visit www.mourningknows.com.

Made in the USA
Columbia, SC
08 March 2020